An Inspector Calls

Michael White

By the Same Author

Paul McCartney's Coat and Other Stories

The Fae Wynrie

Vallum Aelium

Here Be Dragons

An Unremarkable Man

Liverpool

The Waiting Room

Anyone

A Challenging Game of Crumble

Into the Light
Book One: Lost in Translation

Into the Light
Book Two: The Road of the Sun

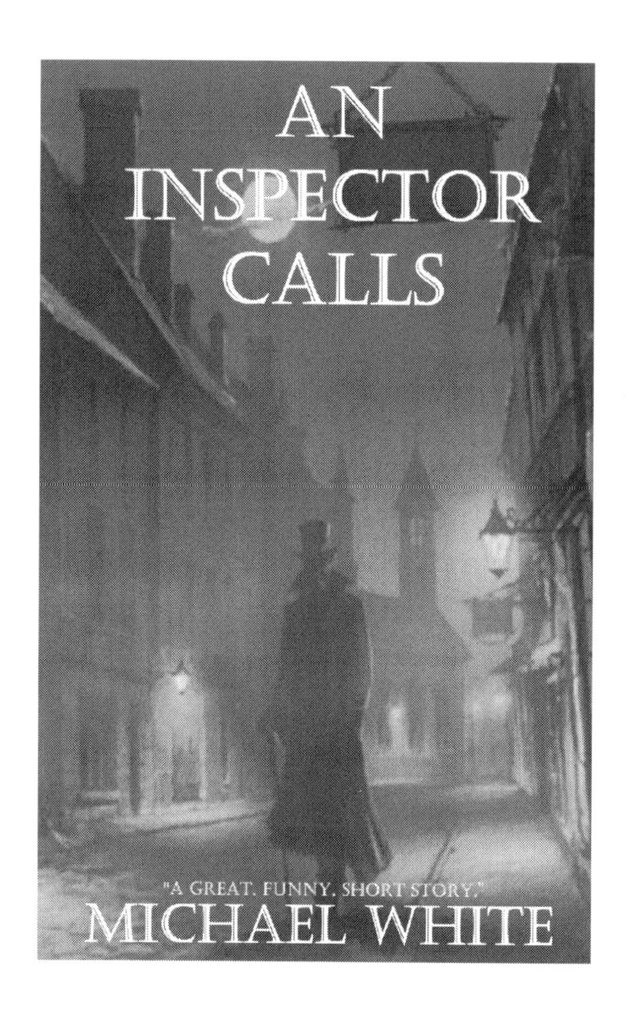
AN
INSPECTOR
CALLS
"A GREAT. FUNNY. SHORT STORY."
MICHAEL WHITE

An Inspector Calls

From the corner of Hesketh Street to the tree lined lane that wound its way towards Grantham's Walk is a swift passage of not more than say, five minutes. Generally a pleasant walk, with trees *just* the right height waving in the breeze, the traffic here is neither too heavy nor too light. In general suburban terms it could be said that it was pretty much an idyllic area. The houses are generally well moneyed, and if the general area could be said to have any problem whatsoever (and it had to be a little bit of nit - picking, it has to be said), it was a small problem. If a problem at all. If forced to express a derogatory opinion, the general consensus would be that the area was just a little *too* middle class; a little bit well, *twee.*

Which in itself is not really any kind of problem at all. If the worst offence that an erring politician could summon was that he was in most opinions, decidedly middle class, or that the military dictator whose latest grand plan involved a lot of: a) drugs, b) lots of money, and c) a certain amount of neat plutonium sitting around doing nothing much at all somewhere in the general area of the Ukraine, (and not necessarily in that order), and if the worst that could be said of such a dictator was that he was, when all was said and done, a little bit, well...*twee*... then the world would most certainly be a much better place. There would certainly be a lot more Ikea stores, for certain.

So, when all is said and one, not a bad area. The trees were nice. The way the sun set just above the crest of the hill as it climbed back towards the town (Strictly May to August - the locals banked on it), all is pretty much as it should have been. Even the lampposts - evenly spaced, cast iron (very old school), were pretty much pillars of good taste.

Down the hill, towards Cressington Gardens, across the small green and there is the village pub. Much has been written about the place of the modern public house in the role of the community, and much has taken place over the last number of decades to change the role of such a building in society. Amongst other things, the advent of the cheap family car, the rise of the out of town shopping centre, the lures used by the modern public house were many. Cheap food and play areas for the family. Dusty the Clown party bags and endless variations of Pizza and chicken nuggets for the kids. The traps were set, and the public fell into them. So the way went, and so the pub - centre of the community, excluder of children, most women and those financially embarrassed - changed. Or most did.

Charles Horse, licensee, proprietor and landlord (his preferred title), of the Bucket and Shovel public house thought that all of this, of course, was complete and utter bullshit. Not for him the modern pub with Sunday lunch for eight pounds, the quiz night on a Monday and Wednesday. No Siree, Charlie ran a traditional public house, and that meant darts, pool, a nineteen sixties / country and western music jukebox and no food whatsoever. (Apart of course from crisps, nuts, pork scratching's and pickled eggs. But they of course, don't really count. (Particularly the pork scratching's and pickled eggs)). As well as these treats there was always fresh sawdust in the bar once a week (whether it was needed or not), tournaments on a rolling basis for darts, pool and a Race night every last Thursday in the month. Charlie believed in the old values. The good old values. And not necessarily family ones, either.

From the outside, the pub looked like any other. This was of frequent embarrassment to carloads of distressed parents on sunny summer afternoons. Keen to offload the kids into the nearest play area, stuff themselves with a good old fashioned pub-produced Sunday roast and the kids with either pizza or chicken nuggets, entering into the Bucket and Shovel could be a salutary experience.

"Excuse me", would stammer a travelling parent, car still outside from where the sound of raucous children could just be heard, "Do you serve Sunday lunch?"

Such a question posed to Charlie would inevitably lead to a smug grin that didn't so much spread across his face as burst its banks and threaten to flood the entire local area.

"Food?" would boom Charlie, pausing to lift a glass from above the bar and polish it with his Cellar man's apron, "Nah," he would pronounce, and that was it. The potential customer would usually stand there waiting for the next bit of the conversation, but it never actually arrived. No directions to the nearest pub that did sell food, no advice on the best route to take; nothing at all, really. Which would inevitably lead to a small-embarrassed silence, and the eventual departure of the slightly disgruntled, if not confused, customer.

Which most entrepreneurs involved in the management of small businesses would find most odd. But that was the thing with Charlie. It was not that he didn't want to serve customers, or that he did not want to make a decent living. Few people would come to the conclusion after examining Charlie's behaviour that he would love to run a chain of pubs. Simply put, he did. It was his dream. But all of his day dream pubs would be run on the same principles. No food. No kids. No play areas - and definitely no designer beers or wine of the month.

The brewery representative had given up on Charlie in this and most other areas now, instead concentrating on the merits of various manufacturers' pickled eggs or scampi fries. It wasn't that Charles Horse didn't want to be successful. It was simply that he didn't want the

20th Century. "Nothing wrong with pubs that have food", he would often comment over the bar to any of his locals who would care to listen. "But not in my pub. Not while I'm the landlord."

By appearances most people would assess Charlie as surly. (This opinion would usually be arrived at after a conversation that would commence with an uninformed customer approaching the bar, speaking to Charlie and vocalising something along the lines of,

"Good evening, Proprietor. May I order a White Chablis, a Taboo Spritzer beer with ice and a packet of Bombay Spice to nibble on. Oh, and whilst you're at it, can I have a look at the menu?" Charlie would smile his wide smile and positively boom,

"We don't do that, I'm afraid."

"Which one?" would smile the customer, thinking to share some mischievous repartee with the landlord.

"All of it." Would pronounce Charlie, and the smile would become just a little wider.

This however, was not the case. He very much believed in the art of giving the punters what they wanted. As long, of course, as what they wanted fell in line with what he was prepared to deliver. This would usually involve some sort of shenanigans to get the potential diner to part with some money for a drink before he told them that the nearest culinary delight they could look forward to was a packet of scampi fries coupled with a small grimy packet that included four Ritz crackers, a Dairy lea cheese slice and a shrivelled pickle onion.

That Charlie had very little trouble in imparting this information had a great deal to do with his rather imposing physical presence. Charlie would often boast that he very rarely had any trouble of any kind in his pub. The fact that the landlord was six foot three and built like one of the steel barrels that contained his relatively mundane real ales could have had a great deal to do with it. The cellar man's apron that none of his customers had ever seen him without, also helped reinforce this opinion. To say that Charlie cut a somewhat imposing presence was like saying that mount Everest was a big mountain.

The Bucket and Shovel was stuck in a veritable Charlie - induced time warp. This revolved around a rather quaint idea of what the local pub should be, and more directly, what it should not be. And the regulars loved him for it. The great thing about a visit to the Bucket and Shovel was that you always knew what to expect. No sudden surprises or arrivals of "beer of the month" to throw you out of your drinking stride. The pub that Charlie ran had very little to offer that could be filed in the cabinet marked, "rare and interesting life enriching experiences", but you did know that you could get a very reasonable price of bitter, and the date of the next race night could be marked very clearly in your social calendar.

Which meant for a brisk trade. Whilst the more consumer orientated pubs struggled to fill more than a few tables of diners on a Tuesday, Wednesday or even Thursday nights, trade for the Bucket and Shovel stayed at a brisk level for most nights of the week. This had a twofold effect on Charlie's running of the pub. One, it made the weekly order for levels of bitter, lager and other consumables less of a gamble and more of a certainty. The second effect was that it gave Charlie a great deal of leeway with the powers that be at the brewery. In an age in which most hostelries were being converted to "Happy Diners" and the like, Charlie was left very much to his own devices, because basically, his philosophy on the day to day running of the pub made them money. Which suited Charlie - and the brewery - just fine.

Charlie remembered several years ago when a new area manager was promoted straight from university, and his subsequent visit to the Bucket and Shovel. An inkling of a smile crept to the corners of Charlie's face at the memory of it. The poor man had arrived with suggestions of designer beers, cocktail happy hours and talk of video jukeboxes. He had left rather hurriedly barely twenty minutes later with a serious loss of self-esteem and a very large and ticklish flea in his ear. He had stuck the job out for another three months or so before leaving to bring the concept of designer ginger nut biscuits to the masses, and was by all counts doing very well for himself off it too, thank you very much.

The fact that the brewery was happy made Charlie very happy indeed. There could be very little wrong with the opinion of the brewery that all in all Charlie was doing a fine job, and was best left to it. Which had the double effect of making Charlie a relatively happy chap as well. So all was well in the Bucket and Shovel. The brewery was happy. The customers were happy. Charlie was happy. Or at least he thought that he was.

But that was before he found the cigarette lighter.

Reflecting back on it he began to wonder just how such a small thing could build into such an obsession. But to consider that he would have to go right back to the beginning. A cold October evening, the regional darts final and cheese and pickle sandwiches.

"It should be cheese and piccalilli, Charlie." Commented Jim, turning his nose up at the buffet sized plate of sandwiches currently doing the rounds at the post darts match finals. To his great pride, the Bucket and Shovel had managed to arrive at the enviable position of overall winners of two of the three competitions for which they qualified. This apparent success however did not put Charlie in the frame of mind for criticism of his post-match buffet.

"Nonsense." Pronounced Charlie, rubbing his down his cellar man's apron. (This apparent habit was something Charlie undertook at moments of indecision, but it was not something he personally felt comfortable admitting to. It seemed to Charlie it was perilously close to admitting a weakness.)

"Cheese should be put with Branston pickle, if it's put with anything at all. Certainly not piccalilli."

To Charlie, the presence of piccalilli in a post darts bash approached something like foreign cuisine, and he certainly was not having any of that at all. Jim pulled a face, which made Charlie think of the thin end of this particularly cheese shaped wedge and carried on its own little train of "over my dead body" thought. Not for the first time Charlie began to ponder the suitability of Jim to head the darts team. Perhaps time to have a word with Simon about next year's season. True, they had not just pretty much cleared the table of all trophies as run off with the tablecloth as well this year, but piccalilli? Bloody hell! It'd be pizza slices next, and then God knows where you would end up.

Charlie placed the large plate down on the pub table and made to return to the bar. "It's bloody Branston pickle, Jim" he announced, in a slightly louder voice than was necessary. May as well begin the undermining sooner rather than later he thought to himself, and in thinking so, turned, leaving a slightly red faced Jim contemplating cheese and Branston pickle, and how they would look placed prominently in a messy crown around about Charlie's head. Charlie knew this of course, and paused on the public side of the bar just long enough for the overhead spotlights to bounce reflectively off the dome of his receding hairline. Presenting himself as a target failed to achieve the desired response from Jim. This began with a plate of cheese and Branston pickle sandwiches being placed around his head and ended with the delightful prospect of Jim rolling around in the gutter outside the pub with a heavily gilded darts statue placed unceremoniously up his arse. Disappointed that Jim didn't seem to want to fix it for him, Charlie returned to the bar to scowl at a few more customers.

Which is when he first noticed the lighter. The bar of the Bucket and Shovel was broadly speaking L -shaped, with the usual arrangement of customers gathering at the crook of the L. The end of the bar was pretty much deserted as usual. This was the end Charlie preferred, where he liked to stand and polish the glasses on his bar apron, and Charlie was as usual unable to decide whether it was because where he stood that made it deserted. Deserted except for the small silver coloured lighter sitting on top of the bar, that is. Charlie picked it up, glancing around, waiting for someone to claim it. Which nobody did. In itself, it was quite an indistinct lighter: flip - top with a small wheel on the side to light the wick.

Flipping the top open Charlie flicked the wheel to light it, and nothing happened. The flint sparked, for sure. But that was it. No flame. Nothing at all. "Probably out of petrol", thought Charlie out loud, and returned the lighter to the bar, leaving it for someone to claim.

Which was the end of it until much later after Charlie had locked up and was about to retire to the flat upstairs. The lighter was still there. Picking it up, Charlie went through the same ritual of trying its fit to his hand, flipping the top open and flicking the wheel in an attempt to light it. It is a sad indication of human nature that anyone finding a stray lighter will always attempt these three things. Usually in that order too. Charlie felt a little peeved at the lighters refusal to play ball, and went to place it under the bar just in case anybody claimed it the next day. "Probably left it because it doesn't work", he announced out aloud to the deserted pub as he noticed for the first time the faded writing on the side of the lighter. The metal case was definitely worn smooth, as of with much use. Which made the letters carved into the case very difficult to read. Holding the lighter up to the spotlight he could just make out individual letters, which seemed to spell out the word "Eribus" in an oddly spaced kind of way. Tiring of the thing Charlie placed it behind the bar and retired to bed.

***

Nobody claimed the lighter the next day. Or the day after that. After a week, despite asking all of his regulars, Charlie decided that the lighter was now his property, but not being a smoker himself, he could think of no particular use for it. But still the writing on the lighter continued to baffle him. Many times throughout the day - during those slack moments - he would find himself pulling the lighter from his pocket and holding it up to the light in an attempt to make out the badly defined letters. With no success. All he could make out was the "Eribus" he had managed to define upon his first cursory glance. Yet he had the distinct feeling that there were a few gaps with more letters on the case, that the letters were there, but just out of reach. After examining it carefully after some time he would invariably return it to his pocket until the next slack moment.

The writing had distracted him for such a while that he had owned the lighter for nearly a month before he tried to light it once again. The flint sparked, but that was all. The lighter plainly refused to ignite, even briefly. The customers of the Bucket and Shovel had begun to catch on to Charlie's seeming preoccupation with the lighter, and had begun to needle him about it. Having passed it around several of them, the general consensus of opinion was still that the writing was pretty much indecipherable, and that it plainly refused to ignite. So Charlie bought a can of petrol fluid and filled it up. Cleaning the noxious liquid from his hands, Charlie flicked the wheel. The lighter sparked, but still did not light. So he replaced the flint. Then the wick. Then emptied the petrol fluid and filled it up again. Then a new flint. Trimmed the wick. Tried again. Replaced the wick. Ignored the catcalls of his customers, "Still not lit that lighter, Charlie? They're only six for a pound at the market. For Christ's sake, go and buy some", and so on. Then back into his pocket for the best part of two days in a serious sulk.

It was at this point that Charlie began to realise that the lighter was beginning to become a talking point in the pub. Customers would ask him about it, ask to examine the illegible writing once more, attempt to convert it to Latin and so on. Never slow to capitalise on a commercial money spinner - as long as it did not involve piccalilli - Charlie began to parade the lighter more frequently, and cajoled his customers in attempts to get the damned thing to actually light. This culminated in it being sent away for a long month to a specialist Tobacconists in Devizes to get it over-hauled. The lighter returned with a specialist engineers report which happily stated that there was no actual reason why it shouldn't light, except that it didn't seem to want to, and the story of the lighter increased in stature a little upon its return. There was also the strange fact that the lighter didn't seem to be from any known lighter company, Eribus or otherwise, and that its origins remained a complete mystery.

Which was great news for Charlie - and good for business too. As the notoriety of the lighter grew, Charlie began to realise that it had the potential to be a nice little earner, with more than the occasional visitor calling in to the pub to look at the thing.

Which is when Charlie had his master plan. Thinking back on it Charlie's commercial brainwave took place over a particularly dull glass polishing session on one cold and wet November morning. It was a logical extension from keeping the lighter under the bar to keeping it on the bar. Knowing the average customer though, drastic measures were called for. As he never tired of telling anyone in particular who would listen, the average punter to the Bucket and Shovel would take the teeth from out of your head, and probably try to sell them back to you as well. Which went some way towards explaining the long metal chain that attached the small lighter to the bar, preventing its movement over more than three foot in any direction, being shackled to the lighter itself by a small iron clamp.

Which was very ingenious, and more than a little bit prominent. Just the thing for getting the punters going over the decision of another pint or not - salt and vinegar or ready salted crisps, etc. etc. Which is just what made the sign above it a stroke of true public house genius. It was a small brass plaque, carefully beaten and deliberately scuffed to make it look as if it were authentically old, rather than knocked up in the back shed a few weeks ago, which it actually was.

It read, "Who so ever can draw a flame from this lighter shall sup free at the Bucket and Shovel for the rest of their days".

And so time passed.

The lighter became a focal part of the pub – and it was taken for sure that anyone who visited made a bee-line for the lighter – in fact, much to Charlie's delight a few of the local rags published articles on it, ensuring Charlie shifted a few more barrels of best bitter and the occasional pickled egg. The lighter, however, remained resolutely unlit. No matter how hard – or softly it was attempted, the lighter just would not light at all. To Charlie it became a novelty, then a piece of furniture, and eventually he would catch himself gazing at it as if he had only just noticed it for the first time, and he would snap out of his reverie and the lighter would become furniture once again.

More time passed.

It could be argued that as far as Charlie was concerned he was definitely in a good place to be. He enjoyed his stewardship of the pub, repelled all challenges to his authority with ease, and continued to make both himself and the brewery happy by shifting beer by the barrel and keeping his supply of pickled eggs and various tasty snacks on the up and up. Still the lighter attracted the occasional punter, but by and large the regulars came to see it as furniture too, which means they stopped seeing it at all. From time to time someone would pick it up, rattle the chain (to which the lighter remained resolutely attached – Charlie was no fool on that score), and perhaps try to light it. To no avail. The crowds of people who had previously pondered on the lettering on it – was that an "E" or a "Y" more or less gave up trying to decipher the text and by and large the lighter was forgotten.

Even to Alf. As the postman to Cressington gardens and the surrounding areas, Alf was partial to a mid-shift elevenses of an alcoholic kind, and as his "walk" as he liked to refer to it took in the Bucket and Shovel, it was not so much a temptation as a certainty that at round about 11 o'clock Alf and Charlie would be engaged in passing the news of the day while Alf delivered the mail and afforded himself of a pint of best (and usually on Fridays) a packet of dry roast too.

To Charlie, in the line of the latest of what seemed to be an on-going series of mysteries, it was the Friday when the letter first arrived.

"Letter for you, Charlie" mumbled Alf through a mouth full of half chewed nuts. Charlie had recently discovered the erasing properties of nail varnish remover on sell by dates printed on packets of crisps and nuts, and therefore the nuts were a little chewier than perhaps they should have been.

"Looks a bit fancy too" said Alf as he passed the envelope to Alf. Charlie couldn't help but agree – the embossed envelope with what looked like hand written fancy writing was certainly a cut above the usual brown envelopes that Charlie reluctantly removed from Alf on what seemed like a daily basis.

Charlie took it from Alf and propped it behind the bottles lined up on the bar. Alf sniffed to himself – no mean feat with as near as damn it half a packet of slightly out of date dry roasted peanuts in his mouth, and of course Charlie knew Alf's curiosity wouldn't be satisfied on his account. He would open the letter later. To Charlie's mind, Alf was far too nosey for a postman, and he made a mental note, though not for the first time, to keep a very careful eye on him. Wouldn't be doing for his bills to be common knowledge, thought Charlie, and risked a quick glance at the letter now carefully nestled between the Gordon's and Smirnoff bottles. It is worth pointing out at this point that although the bottles themselves were genuine, the contents most definitely were not. Charlie subscribed to the view that although punters were prepared to pay a little bit extra for the known brands of certain types of spirits, it wasn't actually in his remit to provide them. Hence both bottles were full of the cash and carry's finest cheaper brands. If, on the rather remote chance that Charlie experienced a pang of remorse on the matter, his argument for the contrary would probably have involved something containing the words, "cheaper", "no-marks" and "osmosis". Luckily this process could not be applied to pickled eggs.

Alf finished his beer and made for the door. It looked as if Charlie was not going to oblige by opening the envelope, despite him casting shifty glances at it out of the corner of his eye, and with that thought Alf made his way back into the high street and the end of his shift.

Charlie waited for the door to swing shut, and then another ten seconds just to make sure Alf wasn't about to (for once in his life) show a bit of intelligence and pop his head back around the corner pretending that he had forgotten something. Charlie eagerly scanned the envelope. The paper seemed pretty good. "Definitely a watermark going on there somewhere", thought Charlie. The writing on it was definitely ink, the letters revealing a careful, flourished hand, the letters large and looped. Being the proverbial half-empty glass, Charlie studied the address. Yup. It was definitely for him. Turning the envelope over a few times he re-read the letters that carefully spelt his name, "Charles Horse Esquire, The Bucket and Shovel" and then the remainder of his address.

Charlie considered putting the letter down and getting on with refilling the pickled eggs but curiosity got the better of him, and he carefully opened the letter. The paper inside was of a similar, if not better, quality of paper than the envelope, and was in similar nearly identical writing to that on the envelope., and was headed with a large gold coloured logo pronouncing the letter was from, "The Elite Guild of Rural Inns, Travelling and Ale Houses". Charlie wasn't sure what a travelling house was, but as it didn't seem to involve piccalilli he continued to read the letter.

Dear Mr Horse,

As the esteemed owners of the Elite Guild of Rural Inns, Travelling and Ale Houses (Hereafter referred to as EGRITAH) we are pleased to inform you that The Bucket and Shovel – of whom you are the rightful custodian as recognised by the above society (EGRITAH) you have been selected to be assessed with a view to becoming a member of our elite society. To this end our fully qualified inspector shall call Monday next at ten am sharp to assess your property and business with the end in mind of adding - at no cost to yourself – your establishment to our elite charter of old fashioned establishments.

Yours……

Charlie scowled a little at the "rightful custodian" – which to him seemed a little bit fancy – but definitely brightened up at the "at no cost to yourself" section. In his mind – Hmm… Monday next. He considered a clean apron and possibly a dust behind the juke box… or perhaps an Elite Guild of Rural Inns, Travelling and Ale Houses would consider a layer of dust a mouse would have to wade through a genuine rural touch? Perhaps he could pass off the slightly aged dry roast peanuts as authentic hand crafted rural snacks? The possibilities hit Charlie like a slow tide edging its way towards a burnt tyre on a beach. The deciding factor however, was the thought of belonging to an *Elite* organisation – almost royalty, was that, and Charlie gave an extra wipe to the mild tap, just for luck.

Monday next came and Charlie ensconced himself at the smoking room window to view the arrival of the inspector. This of course, was Charlie's favourite position, affording him a view not only of the area surrounding the pub but also the street running past it in both directions and therefore also up and down the hill. At the very least this would give Charlie the chance to appraise the inspector for a few seconds as he approached the pub. He was very big on judging people by appearance, was Charlie – and he relished the chance to have a look before the inspector arrived.

Which was odd. At precisely ten o'clock (Charlie's watch was never wrong – and his obsession with getting the time *exactly* right was bordering on OCD) there was a loud knock on the door. Three loud raps, one after another. From the window the only place Charlie could not see was the pub door, and yet he had not seen anyone approach the door at all. As he was pondering this there followed a further three loud raps, and Charlie scuttled across the lounge shouting, "Coming… hang on" and opened the door.

"Good Morning" pronounced the inspector in what was a decidedly deep voice. "An inspector has called." he said and put the somewhat ornate cane he was obviously knocking on the door with back by his side, leaning on it lightly. Charlie was good at appearances. He could tell, for example, the sell by date on the back of a packet of crisps from the front of the bag, and not much got past him, as many of his ex-customers could clearly attest to.

"You need to invite me in" said the inspector, looking up at Charlie with a broad grin. Charlie was, however, very much in a state of shock. It wasn't the deep resonant voice of the inspector or the fact that he clearly bashed his door with his cane at least six times (both clearly banning offences in Charlie's statute book) but the fact that the inspector was – Charlie grasped for a politically correct phrase in a non-politically correct brain – and decided the inspector was... well, at best, oddly dressed. What looked very much like a sort of business suit over a pair of knee high black boots and a hat that was … sort of… well it had a feather in it anyway. Oh, and he was - at best – about four feet tall.

"Glitz is the name" said the diminutive inspector, and Charlie stood aside and invited the inspector in. Glitz stood in the entrance of the pub and surveyed the lounge, removing a small monocle from an unseen side pocket and peering about him.

"*EGRITAH* standard visit" pronounced Glitz, and spun on the spot, taking in the pub entrance in a complete 360-degree manner. "Any vampires, loose demons, headless horsemen or piccalilli about the place?" asked Glitz.

"Shouldn't think so" mumbled Charlie, checking off the list in his mind. "Especially the piccalilli." Charlie felt much more confident about the last part of this, his not having piccalilli being a definite sanctuary in a conversation that seemed to be swiftly in danger of running off the rails.

"Excellent" pronounced Glitz, removing his (decidedly green) jacket and feathered hat, passing them to Charlie to hang up. Charlie presumed this was what he wanted as Glitz pointed his cane at the coat stand and from somewhere out of an unseen pocket pulled a large clipboard and a pen. Squinting over the top of the clipboard - Charlie decided that not only was the inspector in possession of a rather large nose but also that his colouring was - perhaps it was the light bouncing off the bottle of (non) Gordon's gin on the bar, or perhaps it wasn't – a definite shade of green in colour.

Charlie hung up the very small, yet heavy coat and waited. Given time to gather his wits Charlie may very well have had something to say about this intrusion into his pub, but Glitz was not giving him time to think about much at all. Well, much that made sense, anyway.

"Shall we start with the cellar?" asked Glitz and Charlie meekly moved behind the bar and raised the trapdoor that was the only way to access the cellar from the inside of the pub. From behind him Charlie could hear Glitz tutting, and mumbled, almost to himself, "No runes, torch lit passages or adornments" followed by what could not be mistaken for anything else but another loud tut. Charlie secured the trapdoor just in time to turn and see Glitz making a large mark on the paper attached to the clipboard with such a flourish that it could not be anything else but a large cross. Presumably in red, thought Charlie and disappeared down into the cellar.

"I'll get the light" shouted Charlie back to Glitz, but the small inspector was already at the base of the steps.

"No need for me" he pronounced in his deep voice and started to sniff loudly to himself. "Slight dampness, no sign of other worldly occupation or coffins. No hoard either, come to think of it."

This was followed by another loud deep tut and what was without mistake another large red cross. "Shall we proceed?" said the inspector and Glitz disappeared back up the ladder. Charlie wearily ascended back to pub level and closed the trap door shut once more. This was most definitely not going the way that Charlie intended.

"Right" said Glitz, taking a table by the snug and settling his clipboard on the table. "Let us continue with a few general questions." Charlie edged his way on to a stool nervously.

Glitz adjusted his monocle and took possession of the clipboard once more. Staring at Charlie he addressed what was presumably the list on his board. "Food?" he asked.

"Nope" pronounced Charlie proudly. "Just pickled eggs, savoury snacks… and dry roast peanuts of course."

Glitz sniffed loudly and somewhat longer than usual. "Can you smell varnish?" he asked, sniffing again.

"No" replied Charlie, colouring slightly. "Probably the blocks in the toilet."

"We'll come to that" muttered Glitz and consulted his list once more. "Theme nights?"

"Definitely not."

"Not even Beltane? "Enquired Glitz, cocking an eyebrow. On such a face this gave him the unfortunate effect of looking as if his entire top lip was going to slide off.

"Erm… still a no" replied Charlie, trying to remember whether Beltane were a male or female pop group. Either way he'd have none of that kind of nonsense in his pub!

"Provisions and vitals for the road?"

"No."

"Stabling facilities – re-shoeing included?"

"Erm…no"

"Waxed candles and dark snugs for the hiding of rogues and smoking of a pipe?"

"No –we do have a smoking room though."

Glitz huffed to himself in dismissal. "Indeed." He added. "I can see it. Quite bright really, all things considered. What about heathen ales and stilled spirits made on the premises?"

Charlie paused, not really liking what he thought Glitz was alluding to.

"Do you mean cocktails?" he asked, finding his teeth clenching slightly in anticipation.

"Not at all" chuckled Glitz. "I was more thinking of wyverns and the like – but no matter."

This was followed by yet another flourish, and no doubt another red cross. Charlie could feel his elite status falling away from him, and paused to do a mental of the number of his customers he had alluded to the Bucket and Shovel receiving a mysterious new award in the very near future.

The number was alarmingly high.

Glitz seemed to reach a conclusion, and placed his clipboard down on the table with a loud thump. Charlie knew it wasn't good news.

"I'm sorry" he started, but looked anything but. "I'm afraid there must be some mistake Mister Horse. *EGRITAH"* (he pronounced it in capitals almost with relish) "seem to have erred on this occasion. I can find no reason whatsoever for our society to include your establishment into our annals. I must apologise for wasting your time. Most unfortunate."

"We have a race night every last Thursday in the month if that helps" said Charlie hopefully, but judging by the look on Glitz's face it most certainly did not.

"I'm afraid that does not quite cut the mustard Mr Horse" he said and pointed with his cane at his coat and hat hanging on at the top of the coat stand like a set of stranded cot sheets. "I'll be on my way."

Charlie grabbed the coat and hat, and much to his surprise helped Glitz on with them.

"Good day, Mr Horse" pronounced Glitz and clicked his heels together. The clipboard vanished and was replaced with a large cigar. Glitz patted his coat as if searching for a match, tutted loudly, and noticing the lighter on the bar leaned across (rattling the chain on the end quite loudly) and lit his cigar with it.

Time stopped.

Charlie stared at the lit cigar. Glitz removed it from his mouth and stared at the lighter. Somewhere in the pub – impossibly far away, but probably in the attic – a pin dropped.

Charlie tried speaking, but his mouth did not seem to be working. Glitz however grasped the lighter, examined it carefully and then reverently placed it back on the bar.

"Oh my." He spluttered. "Mr Horse, this is a most extraordinary turn of events!"

Glitz seemed like a changed person. He almost ran to the door, the monocle popping out of his eye and dangling on its chain. Jumping up he pulled the door open, turned to Charlie and almost yelled, "We shall be in touch, Mr Horse – oh yes, indeed – we shall be in touch!" And the door slammed shut. There was about ten seconds of silence before the door edged open again and Glitz's head edged around the gap. "Your dry roast nuts are off, by the way" he grimaced, and was gone. Charlie stared at the lighter, stared at the door, waited for the cleaners, and went to bed for three days.

Charlie soon regained his composure though he noticed that despite the strange turn of events the lighter was back to being able to be lit once more. He tried it sporadically at different times of the day, a combination of cigars and cigarettes, but to no avail. Some of his customers wondered (quietly amongst themselves, it must be said) at the slightly nervous tic Charlie seemed to have developed over the last week or so, but no explanation was forthcoming.

Time passed.

A number of weeks passed before Alf sidled in bearing a large envelope with curiously familiar handwriting on it – quality paper and all. Alf knew better than wait for Charlie to open it, but to his surprise, Charlie tore the letter out of his hand, quickly opened it and began to read. The smile on Charlie's face spread like a rising moon – not at the large gold headed charter enclosed in the envelope (which would soon take pride of place behind the bar) but at the contents of the inspector's report. To the casual observer Charlie had just banned the entire cocktail swilling classes, or banned the word "family pub" from the English language.

But the report said it all.

An Inspector Calls

The Bucket and Shovel is a strange place – quiet and off the beaten track yet close enough to attract the attention of the masses from the city. The premises themselves are over-looked by the amenable and appropriately named Charlie Horse who presides over his residents with a confidence befitting his stewardship. We arrived on a non-market day and Mr Horse was kind enough to show us around his premises.

Sadly, the dry roasted nuts are not quite up to scratch, but I did notice a feast of pickled eggs ensconced behind the bar. This could however be the Bucket and Shovel's finest point. The smoking room is decidedly light, the cellar totally devoid of any disembodied spirits or dragon hoards. The stables are non-existent, and I noticed no stable boys or serving wenches to hand, though perhaps we were a little early.

The beers are workmanlike and functional, the conviviality of the host at best obscure, and the host in question obviously thinks Beltane is a rare and terrible disease. The redeeming point however, and this is beyond all doubt, explaining surely the reason that all fine peoples of all realms to make their way there as a matter of priority to enjoy the Bucket and Shovel as it should be enjoyed, is...

"The Great and Mighty Excalibur that is tied and attached to the bar there."

SAMPLES.

NOW READ ON…

A Spoon Filled with Sugar

If you want to find number eighteen Cherry Hill Lane all you have to do is to ask a policeman when you spot one. He will push his helmet to one side, scratch his head as if considering your request carefully and then he will point his white gloved hand and say, “First to your left, take a second right, sharp right again and you are there. Good morning.” If you press him further however then no doubt he would be more inclined to inform you of the recent terrible deeds that have taken place there. He may even remember to whisper details of the terrible black soot marks on the pavements outside of the house, and the fact that even the heaviest of rain showers (and London has lots of those; thunderstorms too) completely fails to wash the soot marks away.

Unlike the policeman however, I do not tolerate mere conjecture, for this is my story and the events that transpired at this address.

I am the master of that house, my name being Geoffrey Berkeley. I am also the head of the trading department that deals with foreign bonds for the bank of Frobisher and Honeywell in the city. I reside at the above address and it is purely through neglect that I can lay at no other door than my own that I found myself on this Autumn morning in search of a new nanny. The previous nanny had left under something of a cloud without even giving notice, which I can assure you caused me a great deal of inconvenience, inconvenience that I could very well do without being a very busy career minded member of my employer, the bank.

Katherine nana, or Kathy nana as my two children, Paul and Susan Berkeley were inclined to call her, gave a damning report on their behaviour, including (amongst other things) a complete lack of respect for her, failure to follow commands and general untidiness and laziness regarding the contents of the nursery.

To say that I was annoyed is an understatement. Apoplectic with rage would be a more fitting description and I had little choice but to place yet another advertisement in The Times for another nanny, this being the fourth in the last three months. In the advertisement. I listed the ideal candidate for the position as requiring a firm hand and to be a disciplinarian, for I felt that my children spent too much time playing and being generally boisterous than learning respect and discipline. What i required was a nanny with a firm hand who was willing to take charge of my brood and give them some moral fibre and obedience to their parents' wishes.

Needless to say, my wife Wilhelmina took her usual lenient stance on my children's upbringing saying quietly to me that it was not such a good idea to have an authoritarian figure looking after them on a daily basis, which beggar's belief if you take Kathy Nana's report to be true.

“Nonsense.” I said to her as I took up a pen and piece of notepaper to draft a list of the requirements that I thought would be essential for a nanny for my two errant children. “Paul and Susan require discipline and plenty of it. There is no point whatsoever in hiring yet another weak willed nanny who will leave us without notice again in a number of weeks’ time. I will not be crossed on this, Wilhelmina!” I shouted and she gave me a glance of reluctant agreement, a look she uses far too often for my liking.

“I suppose you know best, darling.” she sighed. “Though do try to hire someone who doesn’t smack them too much.” I snorted at this.

“Well, Kathy Nana didn’t seem to smack them at all, and look where that has led us!” I surmised. She looked away and I noticed a small piece of paper in her hand.

“What is this then?” I asked as she passed the irregularly folded piece of paper across to me.

“The children have made a note of requirements of their own.” she said, smiling.

“Have they indeed?” I laughed, unfolding the piece of paper to reveal their scruffy handwriting inside. “Look at this handwriting, Wilhelmina!” I protested, waving the paper at my wife who just raised an eyebrow in some unspoken protest I chose to ignore. I glanced at the note again in irritation. “What does this word say?” I said and was surprised as Wilhelmina snatched the paper from my hand.

“Disposition.” she said, though I swear she crossed her eyes attempting to work it out. I sniffed angrily. “Quite a word for a child to use.” I said, not entirely displeased to see that that was what it actually said. “Though if it were a little clearer it would be all for the better I should imagine.” I continued to read the note and was quite frankly appalled by what it contained. “Rosy cheeks?” I spluttered. “Play games!” I think perhaps I need to take matters into my own hands, Wilhelmina! I shall personally supervise the appointment of a new nanny myself!”

"Quite so." said my wife, and with a flourish I tore the note up and threw it into the unlit fireplace, the pieces of paper scattering about the grate.

"I expect the new nanny to mould our young brood into outstanding, and more importantly, well behaved children." I glanced into the fireplace once again. "Preferably with excellent handwriting!" I snorted, and lit my pipe.

Within a few days I had attended the offices of The Times and gave them the advertisement I wished them to run. Needless to say it included no mention of disposition, cheery or otherwise, and certainly did not contain any mention of games or anything of the like. A few choice phrases it did contain included, "firm", "able to give commands", "no nonsense", "traditional", "discipline" and "rules". All in all, I was very pleased with its contents. The time and date and my address were contained in the text and that the interview process was due to start at eight am on the following Monday, which was tomorrow. I had arranged for a day's holiday with my employers at the bank, though I had brought home with me several items of non-confidential paperwork that I would complete later on today, to give me a head start as it were upon my return to work on the Tuesday.

Anticipating having to interview prospective candidates gave me a spring in my step, and I relished the opportunity to do so the next morning. I retired to bed early on Sunday night and slept fitfully enough, though I was woken in the early hours by a loud moaning, no doubt from the wind rushing down the chimney. The thought crossed my mind that perhaps the chimney was overdue a sweeping but it was just a fleeting idea and giving it no more thought I returned to sleep and from that point onwards slept very soundly indeed.

The next day I rose early and attended to my appearance, dressing as one would expect for an employer who is seeking to take on a new member of staff. As is my habit I looked out of the window at the house opposite and took note of the wind direction by examining the weather vane on the rooftop of a house along the street.

"Ah-ha there is a change!" I exclaimed as one of the servants scurried past. I fear I may have startled her as she dropped the linen she was carrying and started scurrying around picking it up again. I never could remember the girl's name despite the fact she has been with us for quite some time, but nevertheless I was not to be deterred. "There is a change coming in!" I continued, tapping my nose as if imparting some secret knowledge. "The wind has changed direction. We have a west wind now." The poor girl continued picking up the linen but looked at me as if I had suddenly grown two heads and a tail.

"Very good sir." she said uncertainly, almost bobbing her head in deference as she continued to pick up the dropped sheets and what have you.

"Warmer times." I finished and she finally picked the rest of the sheets up and made to continue on her way. I maintain a small retinue of servants to accommodate the household in the fashion that I have become accustomed to: a cook of course, a few chambermaids and the like, though I have no real need for a butler as such. No, I live within my limits and prefer to staff my house accordingly. A cook is most surely required, as are the maids, but a nanny is an absolute essential. Without someone in charge of the children chaos is sure to ensue.

"Very good sir." The maid repeated, whatever her name was. "Very good." Sniffing at her apparent lack of understanding I made my way downstairs and took breakfast. Taking up the newspaper I scanned the classified section and carefully read the advertisement. Pleased to note that there were no typographical errors I put the newspaper back on the table and crossed to the window by the front door and gazed out at the road outside, pleased to note that there was a long line of ladies who were obviously nannies (their dour dress sense and general air of disappointment marked them out easily) standing on my doorstep. Even more pleased with myself than before I continued back to the breakfast room and indulged in some tea and toast. I had another fifteen or so minutes to fill as I had no intention of starting the interview process any earlier than I had stated. It was precisely eight o'clock or not at all!

I was just commencing on my second cup of tea when I saw a bright flash of lightning from outside. This was followed three seconds later (I counted them) by a low rumble of thunder. "Three miles away!" I said out loud before continuing to eat the toast as a heavy downpour began to fall outside. This lasted a mere moment or so and then the windows of the house more or less all rattled in unison as a huge gale blew down the street. I swear even the front door shook!

Thinking it strange that the weather was so volatile, what with the wind changing and all I crossed back to the hall and glanced out of the window to check the wind direction once again. I believe that it still said a west wind, though I cannot be sure as I was distracted by the fact that the long line of prospective nannies outside of the door seemed to have vanished! The sky was still overcast, thick black thunderheads rolling across London, though the rain by now was elsewhere. "Perhaps it was clearing the air" I thought as another flash of lightning lit the darkened street, followed shortly after by more thunder. Two seconds this time. Two miles away. I casually glanced at what appeared to be a discarded umbrella lying upon the doorstep. "How careless" I thought, dismayed that all of the nannies had disappeared, though it did cross my mind that if they were scared enough to run away from a little storm then they were obviously not of good enough stock to discipline my children! As I stood there gazing down the street there was another roll of thunder and one second later a pure blue and white bolt of forked lightning struck the road outside my house and I blinked at its ferocity.

When my sight cleared however I was startled to see a small figure dressed all in black standing in the street exactly where the lightning had just struck! I am sure I was not but I must have been mistaken of course. As I watched the figure crossed the pavement and made for my front door. She was as I noted, dressed all in black, carrying a large carpet bag and an umbrella which despite the threat of rain was completely folded up. As she strode purposefully up to the door and rang the bell I took the opportunity to observe her. She was of uncertain age, a tight bun of hair pulling her features into sharp relief, giving her a severe and impatient look. As I stood behind the curtain she turned and smiled at me as if she knew I was there! I pulled back from the window not concerned about being caught in her gaze, but of shock as I looked at her teeth. They were thin and looked sharp, almost like that of some kind of animal predator.

Impatiently she turned and rang the doorbell once again. I was about to rush back down the hall and take a seat in my study when I sighed at the lack of action of anyone actually coming to open the door and so as I was actually adjacent to it I opened it myself.

"Yes?" I impatiently asked the woman stood on the doorstep as with a display of rather bad manners she pushed past me and entered the hall. To my surprise she hurriedly placed her umbrella in my coat stand and turned to face me.

"Mister Berkeley?" she asked quite firmly. I was rather taken aback and so was rather stuck for a response only other than to agree.

"Yes?" I replied as she raised an eyebrow at me.

"Mister Geoffrey Berkeley?" she asked even more forcefully, and I found myself agreeing.

"The same." I stuttered and she sniffed loudly and walked into my study where I was forced to go chasing after her.

"I am your new nanny." she said, removing a glove from one hand and sitting down in front of my desk.

"Well I rather think that I shall be the judge of that." I said, gathering my wits as she smiled again, though thankfully this time with her lips closed.

"Indeed." She continued, ignoring me completely. "I shall require every second Wednesday afternoon off" she finished as I picked up my pen.

"References?" I asked in a daze.

"I make a habit of never giving references." she said with a stare. "A very old fashioned way of doing things if you ask me." My mind went blank. I am not quite sure what happened. Mayhap it was a stale piece of toast or an egg that was not quite up to standard, but I felt hot under the collar and dizzy. As if from a distance I found myself agreeing to her terms. Then the sound cleared as if a bubble had popped and I found her staring at me again as if I were some kind of insect under a microscope.

"Are you quite well?" she asked suddenly and the truth of the matter is that at that point I didn't feel very well at all, though I did find myself protesting that I was in extremely rude health indeed, though she did continue to stare at me as if she knew that I was not telling the entire truth.

"I think I shall put you on a week's trial." she smiled. "I should be sure by then..."

"A Spoon Filled with Sugar" is available from Amazon on the links below.

SAMPLES

Here are a few samples from some of my other stories available on Amazon.

A challenging Game of "Crumble".

"You can't trump the milkmaid with the farmer!" Sighed Old Mother Alice as Mister Crisp placed his "Farmer" card down face up on the fallen over gravestone with a thump.

"Can." said Mister Crisp sulkily as he adjusted his slightly battered top hat back onto his head. As he shuffled his legs on the gravestone upon which he was sitting the wind caught his long black coat, trailing it out behind him in a dramatic manner. Mister Crisp paid it no heed, which was no surprise as the coat appeared to be quite badly burnt, as in fact did Mister Crisp too.

Given the wind was high and blew loudly about the night shrouded graveyard, it was little surprise to any of the five gathered about the upturned tombstone they were using as a table, that Mister Crisp's coat was prone to fluttering about his somewhat blackened form in even the slightest breeze. It would be a reasonable conclusion to deduce that upon this cold and windy All Hallow's Eve it had no chance of staying buttoned at all.

Old Mother Alice squinted at Mister Crisp, her mouth moving wordlessly as if she was chewing something. Her witch's hat and tattered long black cape in contrast did not move in the wind at all. They wouldn't dare.

"If you are going to cheat I am calling it a night dear." she sniffed and the tall skeleton sitting opposite her turned to face its bare skull directly at Mister Crisp. There was a distinct feeling that there was an eyebrow being raised somewhere on the skeleton's face but of course it did not show on the pale white in any shape or form whatsoever.

"Oh alright then." sighed Mister Crisp, picking the card up from the table and replacing it with another.

"Crumble!" shouted Old Mother Alice loudly, banging a new card down onto the gravestone table, making Mister Crisp, the skeleton, an ostentatiously dressed tall man in what appeared to be a cloak more likely to be worn when attending the theatre or an opera, and the small pale man gathered about the makeshift table jump in the air almost simultaneously.

"Woo… woo… woo…" said the thin pale man and as he settled back onto the gravestone he may or may not have been sitting on. The moonlight shone through him, the pale light seeming to catch his face. He looked indistinct; ethereal; out of focus almost.

“Don’t start!” said Mister Crisp, addressing the indistinct figure directly. “Talk properly or don’t talk at all.” The ghostly figure ceased waving its sleeves about almost instantly and the cards laid out in front of him floated down to the horizontal gravestone, revealing his hand.

“Pity that.” said a reedy voice from the shadowy figure. “I nearly had a full hand of blacksmith’s there.” There was a sigh that echoed into the night a little more eerily than was perhaps necessary and the fifth figure at the gravestone shuffled on his makeshift seat and threw his cards down on the table too.

Dressed in a long black cloak that had a collar that covered the back of his head completely he seemed to be immaculately dressed, a stiff white tuxedo shining in the moonlight, long tapered dark trousers and expensive shoes finishing his outfit. He had a slightly aristocratic bearing, as if he were finding the very air he breathed distasteful to his liking. Accordingly, whenever he raised his face he also gave the distinct impression that he was looking down his nose at the same time.

“I ‘ave ‘ad yet another ‘and not to my liking” he said sharply. “Von milk maid, a train driver and an endless succession of chimney sweeps.” He paused for a second as if lost in thought. “Perhaps ve should raise the stakes?” He shivered involuntarily at the use of the word but Old Mother Alice was shaking her head.

"No, Count." she said. "It's a fenic a hand or nothing. I am not losing my petticoats because you can't find a hand of milkmaids and that's the end of it."

"Iv only..." murmured the Count, apparently relishing the idea and the skeleton turned to face him for a second and then also placed his cards on the fallen gravestone in what may or may not have been a desultory manner. It was quite difficult to tell really.

"Another hand?" asked Old Mother Alice as she gathered the cards from the gravestone that was doubling up as a table. All present looked to be in agreement, the Count nodding agreeably, the skeleton nodding, Mister Crisp murmuring a word of acknowledgement, and the ghost gave a small excited "oooo".

A Bad Case of Sigbins

Wallace Barrington's distinction to fame came not from his vast (and some would say *encyclopaedic)* knowledge of the great and revered English garden and all of the pests, bugs and blights that would threaten it, but from his remedies for those same things, his reputation for curing of said problems was at worst much valued by the villagers of Nether Compton, and without doubt equally thought highly of throughout the entire county of Oxfordshire, if not in fact the entire country.

It was Lady Spiers-Faulkner who had first mentioned the greatest challenge of his horticultural consultative career when she had burst into his store one morning, mouth agape, all umbrella and Macintosh.

"Something's at my ruddy pumpkins, Barrington!" she had declared, and cast a look at poor Wallace that gave him no doubt that he was expected to get to the bottom of the affair, and to get there as soon as he was able.

If not sooner.

"Slugs or snails are the most common threat to the pumpkin I usually find, Lady Spiers-Faulkner."

Said Wallace. "Ninety-nine per cent of the cases I have come across it is usually one of those two."

"Must be ruddy big slugs then." She had sniffed testily, "Holes are hand sized and appear overnight. My groundsman has informed me that five of the bloody pumpkins are ruined so far. I fear it will spread if not arrested straight away. I shall expect you at three o'clock sharp, my man." She finished and hurriedly left.

Wallace sighed under his breath. Being the premier consultant in the local vicinity of all things horticultural made him somewhat at the beck and call of any of the local landed gentry who usually expected him to drop the running of his shop and attend their premises with little or no warning. Usually with no payment for his time either, he concluded grumpily. Though this was not always the case, Lady Spiers-Faulkner having been particularly generous in the past.

Wallace's shop was his fame but sadly not his fortune. He had been the proud proprietor of the local village gardening shop for nearly half a century now, ever since he was but a young man, and as his tenure of the shop drew longer so did his advice and experience increase. He made a good honest living from the place, but it was never going to be enough to retire on and so he just kept on going.

The shop itself was looking a little dated now, the wooden counters and shelves from another time. His till was non electric too, and he had very little room to manoeuvre on stock levels, though he usually relied on the basic staples any good gardening store would never run out of. (Slug pellets, tomato food, tools and so on.)

Which could of course be picked up in any major supermarket these days too. Yet still he had a good reliable trade and this was purely down to his knowledge of the plants and vegetables grown nearby, but also what to do when things started to go wrong.

Every summer someone would bring him in a leaf for example and ask if whatever was eating it was either a slug or a caterpillar. (Slug for inside outside of the leaf, caterpillars the other way around.) It was the little things he found to be of use and in these he excelled. Of course from time to time he would need to go and look, and it was for these visits that his reputation grew. There was the strange case of the Right Reverend Frinton-Smith's African slugs for example, or the butterfly moth that very nearly ruined an entire orchard on the property of the Ferry Munstock

Corogan's. The latter had been a close call. After all, who would have suspected so much could be achieved with a small piece of ear wax, a stray piece of cotton and a match. Yet it had sufficed, and so Wallace's reputation for consultative detective work in the field of horticulture slowly grew.

It could be argued that the increase in the regard of his horticultural expertise was directly linked to the appearance of his store, for whilst one grew the other diminished. Yet his customers actually seemed to like this, if not expect it. He very rarely put anything in his shop windows for example and his shelves inside the shop remained resolutely unstocked. Everything was below the counter, though it had been a long long time since he had seen the riddles. Where they were was as complete mystery to him.

Bee's Knees

You are flying above a large garden, floating in a warm Summer's breeze. The air is dusted with pollen which blows through the air as you soar high above the ground below. Looking down you see the garden is surrounded on all sides by a large wooden fence and there is a house to the north. There is what looks like a small copse of trees beyond the house off to the north and a pond to the south. You can move in all directions.

You have 0 out of 100 points and your rank is grub.

What Next?

I look at the screen in anticipation. I ordered this game a few weeks ago, sending off my cheque through the post after I read a glowing review of it in Crash magazine. It definitely took its time getting here though I am ready to play it now. Text adventures they call them. Descriptions of worlds of imagination into which you enter compass directions and give commands to the computer to complete puzzles and solve the game. Fantasy worlds, science fiction, detective stories. There are all kinds of stories. I love them! Lots of people do too - I'm not unusual in that respect, though I do hear some people can love them just a little bit too much. Even heard of one guy wearing a cloak while he plays them, which is a little bit too far, even for me! I look at the opening description. No clue there and so I decide to have a look around the first few locations or "rooms" first.

So here we go. Looks like the game loaded pretty quickly, even if I did leave the cassette tape running while I made a cup of tea. I have the computer laid out on the table in front of me and the afternoon is mine so let's see how far I can get. I can move in all directions, eh? I will try south. Typing out the letters on the spongy Spectrum keyboard I enter my command.

Move South.

You are flying just above the garden now, skimming the plants and shrubs that form a hedge around what looks like a small stone path that leads both north and south. The house is to the north, a large white painted cottage with what appears to be a thatched roof standing next to a small well. There is a shed to the east and a pond to the south, over the surface of which you can see numerous small ticks and flies skinning off the surface of the water.

What Next?

Looks like lots of places to go. Might try the shed but the well sounds kind of interesting too, and there's always the house, that that may prove to be dangerous to a bee I suppose. Well if nothing else at least I am thinking like a bee now, ha! I wonder sometimes if I am spending too much time on these games, but you know? I kind of enjoy them. It's a bit like a crossword puzzle in 3D, or a mind game perhaps. I take another sip of tea. Maybe I will get a biscuit in a minute. Drink's too wet without one so they say. I will try going east to have a look at the shed.

Move East.

A huge shed rises above you here. There is a small wooden knot in the door that you should be just able to squeeze into the inside of the shed through, whilst the path leads back to the garden west. You can also go up to the roof of the shed or down to the ground. There is a large sign on the shed door written in what appears to be white paint. The knothole in the door looks as if it may be dark inside but above you the sky is blue and the breeze is blowing in a leisurely fashion. You can move in, up, down and west. You can also see some pollen.

What Next?

Paul McCartney's Coat

Old Todd was a right old card - I've never met a bloke before or since who was more up for a laugh, I can tell you! But now he's gone and passed over I can tell you a secret he told me years ago, and as far as I know, I think probably it's only him and me that knows all about it. Course, he ain't telling now so it's up to me. This is what he did.

Best place to start would be with the music. Todd was a bugger for it. Rock and roll, pop. Strictly sixties stuff. None of this bloody head banging boom boom boom that seems to be all you can get these days. No idea what's going on in kid's heads listening to that kind of crap! Gives me a right old headache, it does. No, for Todd It had to be sixties music. Golden age, he called it, and he had no shift at all with anything that came after that. Used to get misty eyed about it, he did. Yeah, music was his thing, and he had a particular soft spot for the Beatles. He knew all the tunes, had all the albums. This was back in the days when they were proper albums you had to put on a turntable to play, and if he'd had a few he would sing along to all of their songs, word perfect. Not note perfect, I'd say! But that was Todd for you, though. Dead keen on the songs even if he couldn't carry a tune in a bucket!

Went to all the concerts too, he did. Not for the Beatles like, they hadn't been in front of an audience for at least a year, and even that was in America. Nice work if you can get as far as I can see, but he said he remembered the early days and he had seen them once or twice back then. I think the way he looked at it was once they got popular you couldn't even hear then playing because of the God awful row of all the girls screaming at them. Pretty much ruined it for Todd did that. Course it looks like it ruined it for them as well!

So Todd was a big fan. He didn't have the bloody Beatles wigs and what have you, but he had all of their albums, all their singles. It looked like he couldn't have been a bigger fan. Well, on the music side, anyway.

All that changed though, on the day that he found Paul McCartney's coat.

Dad Comes to Visit

Now this must have been a Monday or maybe a Wednesday. Actually, it was Wednesday because it was fish and chips and it is always fish and chips on a Wednesday, see. Dai came down the stairs and sat on the couch with a right old strange expression on his face. I was watching a bit of telly at the time. Can't really remember what. Anyway I said to him, "What's up with your face then, Dai?" He looked at me in a kind of odd way and said, "Well now Gwen I don't want to worry you but your Dad is sitting on the bed upstairs, like." Now I laughed out loud at this and swore at him for a bit, which made him look kind of really pissed off. Well, sort of.

See, my dad has been dead about eleven years now. IU knew the date so well as it was three years after my ma had died. Not that there was much chance of forgetting, Therefore, I concluded, there was not much likelihood that he was sitting on the bed upstairs. So, wondering what he was up to I decided to play along. "What's he doing then?" I giggled, and for truth this seemed to make Dai even angrier. "He's not doing nothing. Just sitting there." Dai paused for a minute and looked quite serious. "I only went in to get a towel like, and he was just sitting there. Turned to me and said, "Hello Dai" and I kind of ran back out of the room. Gave me a right fright, so it did."

It was only then that I realised that Dai's hair was still wet. Turning off the Telly I stomped out of the room. "Alright then" I called to him as I went up the stairs. "I don't know what you are up to but I will play along for now. I'll just go and..." and when I opened the bedroom door there he was - my dad that is, sitting as large as life on the bed. Only thing was I could see the lamp on the other side of the bed right through him. I felt the hairs on the back of my neck standing up, and that's the truth. "Hello Gwen" he said, smiling. "Hello dad." I replied, feeling kind of strange inside, "what are you doing here then?"

The Ghost Next Door

Me dad use to say that in Liverpool there was always a ghost next door. As a kid I spent many a dark night huddled under the covers in case the ghost from next door decided it liked our house better, because we didn’t seem to have our own ghost so there must definitely be one at number eleven. But as I grew up I began to realise that what he had really meant was that Liverpool as a city was full of stories about ghosts. Scousers love stories, of course, and if they include a ghost or something unexplained happening, all the better. I suppose it's that mix of Irish and Welsh as well as God knows what else. It just seems to invite tall tales.

Dad even had a tale of his own. When he was a kid him and his mates used to play down by Garston docks and there was an abandoned warehouse there that was pretty much just bits of roof left with no walls at all. Just a few metal beams holding what was left of the roof up. Bloody health and safety would have a fit at the thought of kids being able to knock about there these days, but when me dad was a kid that was where they used to play. There was even a little watchman's hut there that was more or less still intact even though it hadn't been used for years and one day they were all playing there when the watchman turned up, and waving at them he went into the hut. Now they all thought that this was a bit odd because, as I say, there was nothing for him to actually watch over any more and after a while they plucked up courage to go and knock on the door to the small shed and ask him what he thought he was doing.

I imagine you probably know where this is heading, because of course when they finally got fed up of knocking on the hut door and opened it the small shed was completely empty. In fact, it looked as if it had been empty for years. There was no other way out of there and they hadn't taken their eyes off it since the old bloke had arrived. Needless to say, they got out of there pretty quick!

So you see, everyone in Liverpool has a ghost story to tell. Everyone seems to have a favourite one, and sometimes they grow in the telling. It would be fair to say that most of them are complete nonsense, but then you never know. You just never know. That's the hook.

An Unremarkable Man

On a petrichorian morning in May we gathered in the old church yard, the air still but slowly warming as the sun rose higher towards noon, the breeze redolent of rain yet filled with a promise of warmth yet to come. The small number of people gathered about the open grave listened intently as the tall man dressed entirely in the darkest of black, a small trilby balanced precariously on his head drew his eulogy to a close.

"Though this you could say of him. Ron was as straight as a die - old fashioned perhaps; some would say old school. But the heart of the matter, and if he were here with us now other than just in spirit, I think he would agree, is the fact that he was to all who knew him an unremarkable man. He never saw a ghost, found treasure buried in the darker wind swept places of the world, nor did he ever own a cat that talked, nor indeed did he have anything remarkable about him at all. That this was the case was his joy, and his secret too. In truth the thing that defined him most in my and many other people's eyes was that *he had no secret.* An unremarkable man, that was Ron. Yet he was loved, and will be missed. Perhaps sometimes that is enough."

The small group of people nodded as the tall man finished his speech, and I thought to myself how unusual the things were that the man had said. I touched the small old coin in my pocket almost subconsciously and smiled, for I knew that some of those things were simply not true. I forced myself back to the present and brought back into focus the soil cast on the coffin, the vicar leading away across the graveyard as I stood red rose in hand beside the grave with a woman who I had met barely an hour before who may - or may not - have been Ron's wife. There would be no cold wind this day; no more rain. Slowly the group departed from the open grave, the grave diggers still out of sight but presumably somewhere near to hand, slowly encroaching on the hole in the ground, no doubt eager to commence filling it in.

"Tsk." muttered the tall woman beside me. She held on to my arm tightly, and I looked back to her, almost as if waiting for permission to cast the rose into the grave.

"An unremarkable man." she muttered, her tone more of irritation than anything. I took a second to examine her once again. The first time I had seen her was when she arrived at the church in a car that looked as if it was from another age. The long black bonnet of the four door Rover fourteen (or so it said on the large, silver polished grill plate) had swung into the churchyard in an almost movie star manner, and once it had pulled to a stop a small shabbily dressed man had jumped out of the driving seat and opened the door for the lady who now stood beside me, holding on to my arm. I thought I saw a tear roll slowly down her cheek but I could not be sure. The woman, who had introduced herself as, "Tish" was old for certain, but certainly not as old as Ron had been. She was still beautiful, her long dark hair only showing slight signs of grey. She was tall, too. Much taller than myself. I would say she was probably five foot ten or thereabouts, and I glanced at her shoes once again, and was still surprised to see that they were quite flat. So she was naturally tall then. The other remarkable thing about her was that she did not seem to be wearing any makeup at all. Yet there was a kind of English Rose quality about her. Dark red, full lips, a slightly upturned nose; large blue eyes. I thought that when she was younger she must have been quite beautiful; and I stopped in my thoughts, realising she still was. The problem I had reconciling mostly was the possibility that she was Ron's wife, for if that was the case then she was obviously much younger than him. That and the fact that I had in all the years I had known Ron never met her at all, though Ron had talked about her all the time.

Tish caught me looking at her and she nodded to me just the once, a slight smile playing across her lips. I turned my attention back to the large hole in the ground and cast the single rose into the grave. It seemed to fall slowly and as it hit the coffin the blood red petals contrasted starkly against the handfuls of soil already cast by the thin group of mourner's moments before. Several petals fell from the flower as it hit the lid of the coffin and spilled across its surface like small drops of blood. The older woman made no sound beside me as we waited; remembering. Perhaps she had much more of Ron to remember than I, for the store of recollections I had of the sweet old man were not many, but they were nevertheless cherished. The thing I remembered most of all about him at that moment in time was how his eyes used to sparkle. It was almost a cross between laughter and a slight edge of mischief playing across his face. It could do nothing else than endear you to him no matter how lost he seemed. As we stood in silence beside the grave I tried hard to recall the first time I had met him. Then it all came back, and I smiled as I remembered…

About the Author.

(Or... "It's all about me.")

Ex-drummer, ex-software author and ex-flares wearer Michael White was born and lives in the north-west of England. In a previous life he was the author of many text adventure games that were popular in the early 1980's. Realising that the creation of these games was in itself a form of writing, he has since made the move into self-publishing, resulting in many short stories and novellas. Covering an eclectic range of subjects, the stories fall increasingly into that "difficult to categorise" genre, causing on-going headaches for the marketing department of his one man publishing company, Eighth Day Publishing.

Having accidentally sacked his marketing director (himself) three times in the last two years, he has now retired to a nice comfortable room where, if he behaves himself, they leave him to write in peace.

In his spare time (!) Michael likes to listen to all kinds of music, and is a big fan of Steven Moffat, whether he likes it or not.

Michael is currently working on several new projects and can be contacted on the links below.

Website:

www. mikewhiteauthor.co.uk

Email: mike@mikewhiteauthor.co.uk

Twitter: @mikewhiteauthor

Amazon Author Page:
http://www.amazon.co.uk/Michael-White/e/B006Y7JHCK/ref=dp_byline_cont_pop_ebooks_1#ASINInjectorTrigger

ALSO AVAILABLE…

ANYONE
MICHAEL WHITE

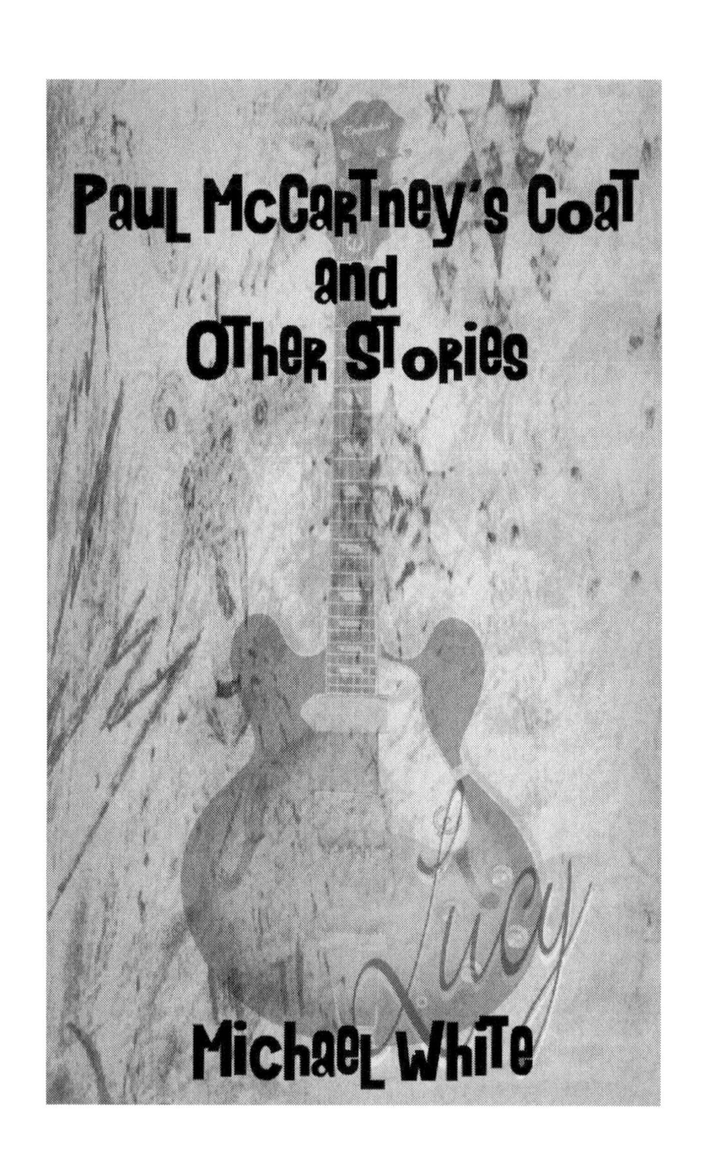
Paul McCartney's Coat
and
Other Stories
Lucy
Michael White

Liverpool
Michael
White

THE VANISHED MAN
A STEAMPUNK ADVENTURE
MICHAEL WHITE

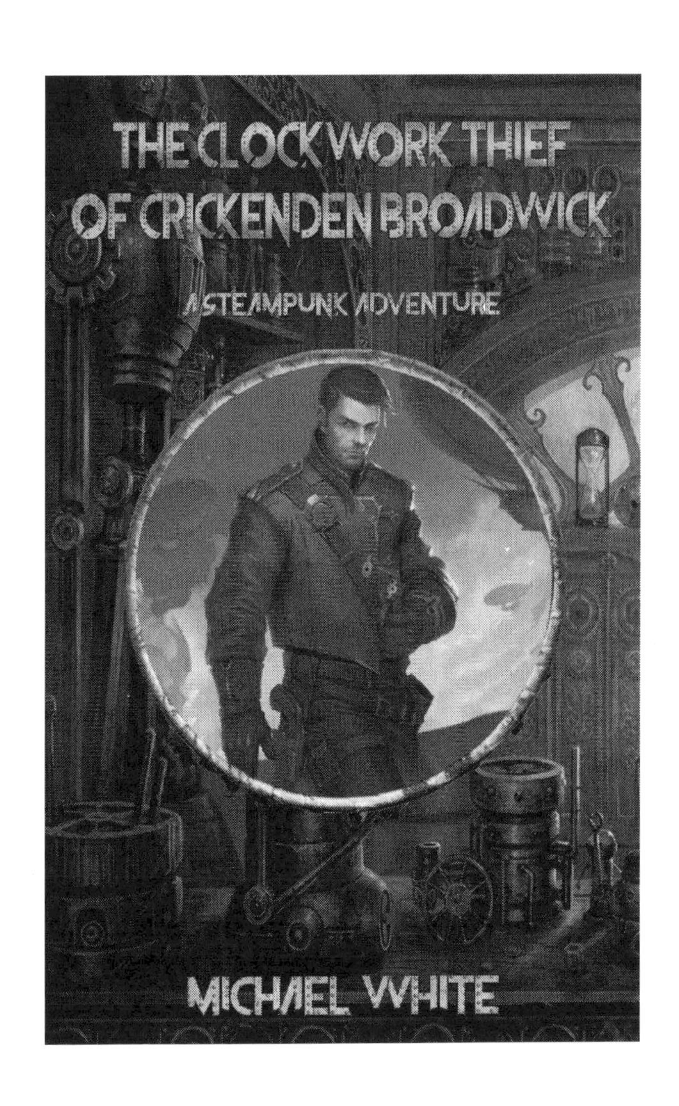
THE CLOCKWORK THIEF
OF CRICKENDEN BROADWICK
A STEAMPUNK ADVENTURE
MICHAEL WHITE

ROMNEY'S DAY OFF
A STEAMPUNK ADVENTURE
SORRY, WE'RE
CLOSED
MICHAEL WHITE

THE ABBOT
BOWTHORPE
DEPENDABLES
A STEAMPUNK ADVENTURE
MICHAEL WHITE

THE ADVENTURES OF
VICTORIA NEAVES
AND ROMNEY

MICHAEL WHITE

Printed in Great Britain
by Amazon